Silhouettes

By

Jerome K. Jerome

British Library Cataloguing-in-Publication Data
A catalogue record for this book is available from the
British Library

Jerome K. Jerome

Jerome Klapka Jerome was born in Walsall, England in 1859. Both his parents died while he was in his early teens, and he was forced to quit school to support himself. Jerome worked for a number of years collecting coal along railway tracks, before trying his hand at acting, journalism, teaching and soliciting. At long last, in 1885, he had some success with *On the Stage – and Off*, a comic memoir of his experiences with an acting troupe. Jerome produced a number of essays over the following years, and married in 1888, spending the honeymoon in "a little boat" on the Thames.

In 1889, Jerome published his most successful and best-remembered work, *Three Men in a Boat*. Featuring himself and two of his friends encountering humorous situations while floating down the Thames in a small boat, the book was an instant success, and has never been out of print. In fact, its popularity was such that the number of registered Thames boats went up fifty percent in the year following its publication. With the financial security provided by *Three Men in a Boat*, Jerome was able to dedicate himself fully to writing, producing eleven more novels and a number of anthologies of short fiction.

In 1926, Jerome published his autobiography, *My Life and Times*. He died a year later, aged 68.

I fear I must be of a somewhat gruesome turn of mind. My sympathies are always with the melancholy side of life and nature. I love the chill October days, when the brown leaves lie thick and sodden underneath your feet, and a low sound as of stifled sobbing is heard in the damp woods--the evenings in late autumn time, when the white mist creeps across the fields, making it seem as though old Earth, feeling the night air cold to its poor bones, were drawing ghostly bedclothes round its withered limbs. I like the twilight of the long grey street, sad with the wailing cry of the distant muffin man. One thinks of him, as, strangely mitred, he glides by through the gloom, jangling his harsh bell, as the High Priest of the pale spirit of Indigestion, summoning the devout to come forth and worship. I find a sweetness in the aching dreariness of Sabbath afternoons in genteel suburbs--in the evil-laden desolateness of waste places by the river, when the yellow fog is stealing inland across the ooze and mud, and the black tide gurgles softly round worm-eaten piles.

I love the bleak moor, when the thin long line of the winding road lies white on the darkening heath, while overhead some belated bird, vexed with itself for being out so late, scurries across the dusky sky, screaming angrily. I love the lonely, sullen lake, hidden away in mountain solitudes. I suppose it was my childhood's surroundings that instilled in me this affection for sombre hues. One of my earliest recollections is of a dreary marshland by the sea. By day, the water stood there in wide, shallow pools. But when one looked in the evening they were pools of blood that lay there.

It was a wild, dismal stretch of coast. One day, I found myself there all alone--I forget how it came about--and, oh, how small I felt amid the sky and the sea and the sandhills! I ran, and ran, and ran, but I never seemed to move; and then I cried, and screamed, louder and louder, and the circling seagulls screamed back mockingly at me. It was an "unken" spot, as they say up North.

In the far back days of the building of the world, a long, high ridge of stones had been reared up by the sea, dividing the swampy grassland from the sand. Some of these stones--"pebbles," so they called them round about--were as big as a man, and many as big as a fair-sized house; and when the sea was angry--and very prone he was to anger by that lonely shore, and very quick to wrath; often have I known him sink to sleep with a peaceful smile on his rippling waves, to wake in fierce fury before the night was spent--he would snatch up giant handfuls of these pebbles and fling and toss them here and there, till the noise of their rolling and crashing could be heard by the watchers in the village afar off.

"Old Nick's playing at marbles to-night," they would say to one another, pausing to listen. And then the women would close tight their doors, and try not to hear the sound.

Far out to sea, by where the muddy mouth of the river yawned wide, there rose ever a thin white line of surf, and underneath those crested waves there dwelt a very fearsome thing, called the Bar. I grew to hate and be afraid of this mysterious Bar, for I heard it spoken of always with bated breath, and I knew that it was very cruel to fisher folk, and hurt them so sometimes that they would cry whole days and nights together with the pain, or would sit with white scared faces, rocking themselves to and fro.

Once when I was playing among the sandhills, there came by a tall, grey woman, bending beneath a load of driftwood. She paused when nearly opposite to me, and, facing seaward, fixed her eyes upon the breaking surf above the Bar. "Ah, how I hate the sight of your white teeth!" she muttered; then turned and passed on.

Another morning, walking through the village, I heard a low wailing come from one of the cottages, while a little farther on a group of women were gathered in the roadway, talking. "Ay," said one of them, "I thought the Bar was looking hungry last night."

So, putting one and the other together, I concluded that the "Bar" must be an ogre, such as a body reads of in books, who lived in a coral castle deep below the river's mouth, and fed upon the fishermen as he caught them going down to the sea or coming home.

From my bedroom window, on moonlight nights, I could watch the silvery foam, marking the spot beneath where he lay hid; and I would stand on tip- toe, peering out, until at length I would come to fancy I could see his hideous form floating below the waters. Then, as the little white-sailed boats stole by him, tremblingly, I used to tremble too, lest he should suddenly open his grim jaws and gulp them down; and when they had all safely reached the dark, soft sea beyond, I would steal back to the bedside, and pray to God to make the Bar good, so that he would give up eating the poor fishermen.

Another incident connected with that coast lives in my mind. It was the morning after a great storm--great even for that stormy coast--and the passion-worn waters were still heaving with the memory of a fury that was dead. Old Nick had scattered his marbles far and wide, and there were rents and fissures in the pebbly wall such as the oldest fisherman had never known before. Some of the hugest stones lay tossed a hundred yards away, and the waters had dug pits here and there along the ridge so deep that a tall man might stand in some of them, and yet his head not reach the level of the sand.

Round one of these holes a small crowd was pressing eagerly, while one man, standing in the hollow, was lifting the few remaining stones off something that lay there at the bottom. I pushed my way between the straggling legs of a big fisher lad, and peered over with the rest. A ray of sunlight streamed down into the pit, and the thing at the bottom gleamed white. Sprawling there among the black pebbles it looked like a huge spider. One by one the last stones were lifted away, and the thing was left bare, and then the crowd looked at one another and shivered.

"Wonder how he got there," said a woman at length; "somebody must ha' helped him."

"Some foreign chap, no doubt," said the man who had lifted off the stones; "washed ashore and buried here by the sea."

"What, six foot below the water-mark, wi' all they stones atop of him?" said another.

"That's no foreign chap," cried a grizzled old woman, pressing forward. "What's that that's aside him?"

Some one jumped down and took it from the stone where it lay glistening, and handed it up to her, and she clutched it in her skinny hand. It was a gold earring, such as fishermen sometimes wear. But this was a somewhat large one, and of rather unusual shape.

"That's young Abram Parsons, I tell 'ee, as lies down there," cried the old creature, wildly. "I ought to know. I gave him the pair o' these forty year ago."

It may be only an idea of mine, born of after brooding upon the scene. I am inclined to think it must be so, for I was only a child at the time, and would hardly have noticed such a thing. But it seems to my remembrance that as the old crone ceased, another woman in the crowd raised her eyes slowly, and fixed them on a withered, ancient man, who leant upon a stick, and that for a moment, unnoticed by the rest, these two stood looking strangely at each other.

From these sea-scented scenes, my memory travels to a weary land where dead ashes lie, and there is blackness--blackness everywhere. Black rivers flow between black banks; black, stunted trees grow in black fields; black withered flowers by black wayside. Black roads lead from blackness past blackness to blackness; and along them trudge black, savage-looking men and women; and by them black, old-looking children play grim, unchildish games.

When the sun shines on this black land, it glitters black and hard; and when the rain falls a black mist rises towards heaven, like the hopeless prayer of a hopeless soul.

By night it is less dreary, for then the sky gleams with a lurid light, and out of the darkness the red flames leap, and high up in the air they gambol and writhe--the demon spawn of that evil land, they seem.

Visitors who came to our house would tell strange tales of this black land, and some of the stories I am inclined to think were true. One man said he saw a young bull-dog fly at a boy and pin him by the throat. The lad jumped about with much sprightliness, and tried to knock the dog away. Whereupon the boy's father rushed out of the house, hard by, and caught his son and heir roughly by the shoulder. "Keep still, thee young ---, can't 'ee!" shouted the man angrily; "let 'un taste blood."

Another time, I heard a lady tell how she had visited a cottage during a strike, to find the baby, together with the other children, almost dying for want of food. "Dear, dear me!" she cried, taking the wee wizened mite from the mother's arms, "but I sent you down a quart of milk, yesterday. Hasn't the child had it?"

"Theer weer a little coom, thank 'ee kindly, ma'am," the father took upon himself to answer; "but thee see it weer only just enow for the poops."

We lived in a big lonely house on the edge of a wide common. One night, I remember, just as I was reluctantly preparing to climb into bed, there came a wild ringing at the gate, followed by a hoarse, shrieking cry, and then a frenzied shaking of the iron bars.

Then hurrying footsteps sounded through the house, and the swift opening and closing of doors; and I slipped back hastily into my knickerbockers and ran out. The women folk were gathered on the stairs, while my father stood in the hall, calling to them to be quiet. And still the wild ringing of the bell continued, and, above it, the hoarse, shrieking cry.

My father opened the door and went out, and we could hear him striding down the gravel path, and we clung to one another and waited.

After what seemed an endless time, we heard the heavy gate unbarred, and quickly clanged to, and footsteps returning on the gravel. Then the door opened again, and my father entered, and behind him a crouching figure that felt its way with its hands as it crept along, as a blind man might. The figure stood up when it reached the middle of the hall, and mopped its eyes with a dirty rag that it carried in its hand; after which it held the rag over the umbrella-stand and wrung it out, as washerwomen wring out clothes, and the dark drippings fell into the tray with a dull, heavy splut.

My father whispered something to my mother, and she went out towards the back; and, in a little while, we heard the stamping of hoofs--the angry plunge of a spur-startled horse--the rhythmic throb of the long, straight gallop, dying away into the distance.

My mother returned and spoke some reassuring words to the servants. My father, having made fast the door and extinguished all but one or two of the lights, had gone into a small room on the right of the hall; the crouching figure, still mopping that moisture from its eyes, following him. We could hear them talking there in low tones, my father questioning, the other voice thick and interspersed with short panting grunts.

We on the stairs huddled closer together, and, in the darkness, I felt my mother's arm steal round me and encompass me, so that I was not afraid. Then we waited, while the silence round our frightened whispers thickened and grew heavy till the weight of it seemed to hurt us.

At length, out of its depths, there crept to our ears a faint murmur. It gathered strength like the sound of the oncoming of a wave upon a stony shore, until it broke in a Babel of vehement voices just outside. After a few moments, the hubbub ceased, and there came a furious ringing--then angry shouts demanding admittance.

Some of the women began to cry. My father came out into the hall, closing the room door behind him, and ordered them to be quiet, so sternly that they were stunned into silence. The furious ringing was repeated; and, this time, threats mingled among the hoarse shouts. My mother's arm tightened around me, and I could hear the beating of her heart.

The voices outside the gate sank into a low confused mumbling. Soon they died away altogether, and the silence flowed back.

My father turned up the hall lamp, and stood listening.

Suddenly, from the back of the house, rose the noise of a great crashing, followed by oaths and savage laughter.

My father rushed forward, but was borne back; and, in an instant, the hall was full of grim, ferocious faces. My father, trembling a little (or else it was the shadow cast by the flickering lamp), and with lips tight pressed, stood confronting them; while we women and children, too scared to even cry, shrank back up the stairs.

What followed during the next few moments is, in my memory, only a confused tumult, above which my father's high, clear tones rise every now and again, entreating, arguing, commanding. I see nothing distinctly until one of the grimmest of the faces thrusts itself before the others, and a voice which, like Aaron's rod, swallows up all its fellows, says in deep, determined bass, "Coom, we've had enow chatter, master. Thee mun give 'un up, or thee mun get out o' th' way an' we'll search th' house for oursel'."

Then a light flashed into my father's eyes that kindled something inside me, so that the fear went out of me, and I struggled to free myself from my mother's arm, for the desire stirred me to fling myself down upon the grimy faces below, and beat and stamp upon them with my fists. Springing across the hall, he snatched from the wall where it hung an ancient club, part of a trophy of old armour, and planting his back against the door through which they would have to pass, he shouted,

"Then be damned to you all, he's in this room! Come and fetch him out."

(I recollect that speech well. I puzzled over it, even at that time, excited though I was. I had always been told that only low, wicked people ever used the word "damn," and I tried to reconcile things, and failed.)

The men drew back and muttered among themselves. It was an ugly-looking weapon, studded with iron spikes. My father held it secured to his hand by a chain, and there was an ugly look about him also, now, that gave his face a strange likeness to the dark faces round him.

But my mother grew very white and cold, and underneath her breath she kept crying, "Oh, will they never come--will they never come?" and a cricket somewhere about the house began to chirp.

Then all at once, without a word, my mother flew down the stairs, and passed like a flash of light through the crowd of dusky figures. How she did it I could never understand, for the two heavy bolts had both been drawn, but the next moment the door stood wide open; and a hum of voices, cheery with the anticipation of a period of perfect bliss, was borne in upon the cool night air.

My mother was always very quick of hearing.

* * * * *

Again, I see a wild crowd of grim faces, and my father's, very pale, amongst them. But this time the faces are very many, and they come and go like faces in a dream. The ground beneath my feet is wet and sloppy, and a black rain is falling. There are women's faces in the crowd, wild and haggard, and long skinny arms stretch out threateningly towards my father, and shrill, frenzied voices call out curses on him. Boys' faces also pass me in the grey light, and on some of them there is an impish grin.

I seem to be in everybody's way; and to get out of it, I crawl into a dark, draughty corner and crouch there among cinders. Around me, great engines fiercely strain and pant like living things fighting beyond their strength. Their gaunt arms whirl madly above me, and the ground rocks with their throbbing. Dark figures flit to and fro, pausing from time to time to wipe the black sweat from their faces.

The pale light fades, and the flame-lit night lies red upon the land. The flitting figures take strange shapes. I hear the hissing of wheels, the furious clanking of iron chains, the hoarse shouting of many voices, the hurrying tread of many feet; and, through all, the wailing and weeping and cursing that never seem to cease. I drop into a restless sleep, and dream that I have broken a chapel window, stone-throwing, and have died and gone to hell.

At length, a cold hand is laid upon my shoulder, and I awake. The wild faces have vanished and all is silent now, and I wonder if the whole thing has been a dream. My father lifts me into the dog-cart, and we drive home through the chill dawn.

My mother opens the door softly as we alight. She does not speak, only looks her question. "It's all over, Maggie," answers my father very quietly, as he takes off his coat and lays it across a chair; "we've got to begin the world afresh."

My mother's arms steal up about his neck; and I, feeling heavy with a trouble I do not understand, creep off to bed.

[The end]

www.ingramcontent.com/pod-product-compliance
Lightning Source LLC
Chambersburg PA
CBHW050319200626
46808CB00023BA/3065